A Note to Parents

Read to your child...

★ Reading aloud is one of the best ways to develop your child's love of reading. Read together at least 20 minutes each day.

★ Laughter is contagious! Read with feeling. Show your child that reading is fun.

★ Take time to answer questions your child may have about the story. Linger over pages that interest your child.

...and your child will read to you.

★ Follow cues from your child to know when he wants to join in the reading.

★ Support your young reader. Give him a word whenever he asks for it.

★ Praise your child as he progresses. Your encouraging words will build his confidence.

You can help your Level 1 reader.

★ Reading begins with knowing how a book works. Show your child the title and where the story begins.

★ Ask your child to find picture clues on each page. Talk about what is happening in the story.

★ Point to the words as you read so your child can make the connection between the print and the story.

★ Ask your child to point to words she knows.

★ Let your child supply the rhyming words.

Most of all, enjoy your reading time together!

—Bernice Cullinan, Ph.D.,
Professor of Reading, New York University

Fisher-Price and related trademarks and copyrights are used under
license from Fisher-Price, Inc., a subsidiary of Mattel, Inc.,
East Aurora, NY 14052 U.S.A.
©2003, 2000 Mattel, Inc.
All Rights Reserved. **MADE IN CHINA**.
Published by Reader's Digest Children's Books
Reader's Digest Road, Pleasantville, NY U.S.A. 10570-7000
Copyright © 1999 Reader's Digest Children's Publishing, Inc.
All rights reserved. Reader's Digest Children's Books is a trademark
and Reader's Digest and All-Star Readers are registered trademarks of
The Reader's Digest Association, Inc.
Conforms to ASTM F963 and EN 71
10

Library of Congress Cataloging-in-Publication Data

Hood, Susan.
Let's jump in! / by Susan Hood ; illustrated by Mike Gordon.
p. cm. — (All-star readers. Level 1)
Summary: A rhyming story about a boy whose friends help teach him to swim.
ISBN 1-57584-320-X
[1. Swimming—Fiction. 2. Stories in rhyme.]
I. Gordon, Mike, ill. II. Title. III. Series.
PZ8.3.H7577Lg 1999 [E]—dc21 99-18494

Let's Jump In!

by Susan Hood
illustrated by Mike Gordon

Reader's Digest Children's Books™
Pleasantville, New York • Montréal, Québec

Let's jump in the pool!
Let's go for a swim!

The kids jumped in...

...all but Tim.

Tim dipped his foot in.

Ooh, it's chilly!

Tim felt scared.

Was that silly?

Tim put his feet in
at one end.

Then who popped up?
Dan, his friend!

Jump in the pool.
Jump in, Tim!

We will help you learn to swim.

Dan helped Tim float...

...and learn the crawl.

Swimming was not
hard at all!

Now Tim can dive

and splash and race.

One day he even
won first place!

Now when the kids say, “Come and swim,”

the first one in is—

guess who—

Tim!

Color in the star next to each word you can read.

☆ a	☆ first	☆ kids	☆ swimming
☆ all	☆ float	☆ learn	☆ that
☆ and	☆ foot	☆ let's	☆ the
☆ at	☆ for	☆ not	☆ then
☆ but	☆ friend	☆ now	☆ Tim
☆ can	☆ go	☆ one	☆ to
☆ chilly	☆ guess	☆ ooh	☆ up
☆ come	☆ hard	☆ place	☆ was
☆ crawl	☆ he	☆ pool	☆ we
☆ Dan	☆ help	☆ popped	☆ when
☆ day	☆ helped	☆ put	☆ who
☆ dipped	☆ his	☆ race	☆ will
☆ dive	☆ in	☆ say	☆ won
☆ end	☆ is	☆ scared	☆ you
☆ even	☆ it's	☆ silly	
☆ feet	☆ jump	☆ splash	
☆ felt	☆ jumped	☆ swim	